THE SPIRITS
OF CHRISTMAS

The Spirits
of Christmas

by

Paul Kane

Black Shuck Books
www.BlackShuckBooks.co.uk

First published in the UK by Black Shuck Books, 2016

978-1-913038-06-9

The Spirits of Christmas

Gareth Powell hated this time of year.

Not because of what it represented; he didn't believe in religion but didn't mind it either. Certainly didn't actively loathe it. Each to their own: if true believers didn't bother him, Gareth was happy enough to leave them alone, too. After all, he had his own religion, didn't he? It was certainly *spirit*-ual... That joke always made him chuckle to himself.

It wasn't because of all the cheer and goodwill, either – although when Gareth looked around at the families shopping, it reminded him of the things he'd lost. That he'd be alone on Christmas morning, just as he had been the last four or five Christmases. Well, not really alone, he'd remind himself whenever he felt like this. He did have company, the kind that would send him to oblivion before the Queen had even settled down to open her mouth, the kind that had been Gareth's only real friend for so long. His *best* friend, one that would never judge him, never demand anything (unless he failed to keep up his end of the deal, that was). Would only ever comfort and support him.

In fact, the goodwill thing actually worked in his favour. People were much more generous at this time, more inclined to treat perfect strangers... like him. If Gareth hung around long enough, they might even think they knew him. An old school friend, perhaps, someone they'd worked with in the past. And he wouldn't say no to their offers to put their hands in their pockets; it helped him conserve his own cash, helped him to fund his own... hobby.

No, he hated this time of year because of how much busier it got in the places he liked to frequent. *The Red Lion*, *The Fox and Hound*, *The Black Sheep* (funny how so many of them were named after animals; maybe it was because, like them, humans were creatures of habit?). It was the one time of year when the people who really didn't drink that much would end up in pubs across the land – following Xmas work parties, or even having them there. It meant that the serious drinkers couldn't move for bodies, couldn't get to the bar for folks ordering Baileys and cocktails with strange names. At Christmas – and New Year, yes, don't forget about that! – it took an age to get served. It was one of the reasons Gareth would come back from the bar with two, sometimes even three, drinks: if a tray was handy, and he could still carry it without serious spillage, navigating around the constantly shifting, fleshy assault course. It would save him both time and trouble. Oh, he knew all the wrinkles after thirty-odd years of getting wrecked.

These same establishments would more than likely be closed on Christmas and Boxing Day, to boot. Any that opened only did so for a few hours so that the owners could spend quality time with their own families (don't think about that, Gareth, have a drink instead). Another reason he tucked himself away on the morning of the 25th, pouring glass after glass, or just necking it from the bottle if he couldn't wait. Watching the parade of feel-good programming transform into a surreal and unintelligible mess in front of his eyes – and one he'd have no hope of remembering when he did finally rouse later on in the day to start his next binge.

But that was a few days away yet, a week perhaps, though it was getting harder and harder to keep track of the date. Or the time, come to that. Gareth screwed up his eyes to squint at the clock on the wall. Ten something; eleven maybe. Christ, he'd better work it out soon in case it was last orders. There'd be a stampede in here when they called that. Satisfied it was a way off yet, he looked around at the crowded public house, taking in details that would only remain in his memory for fleeting seconds. No matter how much he attempted to hang on to them, it was like trying to wrestle fog.

At various tables, couples – some of them only just hooking up tonight – were growing increasingly more intimate, slurred words and sloppy kisses being exchanged; they probably wouldn't be the only things exchanged before the night was out. Gareth zoned in on one particular pair: a balding, ferret-faced man who had been chatting up a woman all evening. A woman so big she looked like she'd crush him flat in bed. He had one hand in her mop of frizzy blonde hair up to his wrist – looked like it was being eaten – and his other on her thigh, stroking the shiny material of her party frock, fingers inching ever higher.

At the fruit machine two lads in jeans and day-glo shirts were shoving money into the thing like they were feeding it, pulling on the handle and watching the painted representations of bananas, oranges and lemons spin by. It came up a win, probably the only one all evening, but they took this and started putting the coins back in again. Gareth thought what a waste that was, when they could be buying more booze. Buying *him* more booze...

A few of the newer patrons, who wouldn't be caught dead in here come January, had put a Christmas song on the jukebox (more money wastage) and had linked arms to sing along with the gravel-voiced pop star who'd probably made more from this one tune being played every festive season than all his other 'hits' combined. It wasn't their normal behaviour, you could tell. And they'd be horribly embarrassed when they saw the photos one of their number kept insisting on taking with his mobile phone... or was he videoing it? Even worse.

Gareth took another long draught of his real ale, then a sip of his whiskey chaser. The combination was delightful. First the sourness of the beer – an acquired taste, but one he'd embraced a long time ago – then the fire on his tongue, down his throat. He shivered involuntarily. The knowledge that he shouldn't really be having any alcohol *at all* made it that much sweeter.

"Bloody doctors," he slurred to himself. "What do they know?" He'd been drinking since he was old enough to hold a glass, first at family events, then secretly on his own. It hadn't caused him any harm in the past. He'd done the whole teen thing, smuggling in booze to school discos, or at parties when people's parents were away. He'd been the cool one, always popular, the life and soul. Later still, on the club scene, at 18-30 holidays, out with his buddies, on the lash and on the pull. It was how he'd met Denise, in the pool at the hotel – she'd looked knockout in that little blue bikini of hers – and, to his surprise, he'd pulled her right there and then.

When they got back home, they'd started seeing each other, and realised they had a fair amount in common: films, books, TV shows.

Going out and having a good time… that was the main one. But then it had all got serious, suddenly. The next thing he knew, they were settling down and she was expecting him to start saving money, to be in from work on the dot instead of grabbing a few with the lads after his shift at the car plant was over. It was his way of unwinding, wasn't it? And, of course, when Denise had fallen pregnant after he'd drunkenly insisted on sex that Saturday when he'd got home from the snooker hall (Denise hated snooker), it had made things even worse. She'd sworn blind she hadn't forgotten to take her pill, but he never really believed her. Just another way of tying him down.

Responsibility – he'd never asked for any of it. Didn't want it. Just wanted another drink, followed by another and yet another.

For her sake more than anything, he'd tried to dry out a few times, especially when she'd nagged him, or argued it had got the better of him. "I can stop whenever I want," he'd snapped. "And I don't need any help to do it, either!" But all evidence pointed to the contrary. Not only couldn't he stop, he was drinking more than ever. Hiding it from her, as well – Denise had no clue just how much. Well, not until she came back from visiting her folks one weekend to find him passed out when he should have been making little Sara her tea.

"Anything could've happened!" Denise had barked at him. It hadn't, though, had it? He had things under control, just like always.

Denise had given him an ultimatum then: the drink, or his family. Gareth still didn't see why he couldn't have both, which told Denise everything she needed to know. She and Sara came second in his life. In his heart. And so she'd left him, taking his daughter with her. She was shacked up with some poncey bank manager now... bastard. Gave Sara anything she asked for (imagine the pile of presents on Christmas morning at their house... no, on second thoughts, don't...), was around whenever she had a problem, not just a disembodied voice on the end of a telephone line – because it hurt too much to see her (because she was better off without him?). Because Gareth saw what she thought of him reflected in her eyes, and that just made him want another drink all the more.

Sometimes, just sometimes, he imagined there was a parallel universe version of himself that had never even started drinking. One who was still with his family, still in a proper house instead of a bed-sit. Still had his job at the car plant, although that really hadn't been his fault – how could he have avoided being made redundant? It had been taken out of his hands (perhaps if he'd put more effort into the work, hadn't been so distracted by the drink – or even *thinking* about the next drink – maybe then they wouldn't have been so keen to get rid of him? Naw; everything happens for a reason, right?). A version of Gareth who hadn't blown most of his redundancy on alcohol and wasn't now reduced to claiming benefits, spending them almost as soon as the money was in his pocket. Wasn't looking at his bank balance – from the same fucking bank the man who was diddling his wife... sorry, ex-wife... worked for – and thinking, *how am I going to pay the heating bills this winter?* Thinking: *it doesn't matter because I can still have a drink to warm myself up.* Or thinking: *when I drink I don't have to think about any of this shit in the first place.*

Gareth shook his head, took another swig of the ale, but this time knocked back the whiskey in one. He considered going up to the bar again, but by the time he got served, it would probably – definitely – be last orders, and then chucking out time. It was too crowded in here tonight anyway. Too difficult to make your way to the bar itself without tripping over other drinkers (or your feet). He might as well head back and get started on that bottle of cheap vodka he had stashed away at his place – or had he drunk that already? No, he felt certain he hadn't... well, hoped he hadn't. With that same hope drunks always have that they've forgotten a bottle or two they'd hidden away for a rainy... snowy day.

Because, as he stumbled to the door and stepped outside, he realised that not only had the temperature dropped while he'd been inside the *Nag's Head* (another animal!), but there had also been a light dusting of snow covering the streets he'd have to pound to get back home. Crap! It was going to be hard enough walking on the pavement as it was, after the skinful he'd had, let alone being unsure of your footing. He could wave down a taxi, but that would mean parting with more money he could use for drink. No, screw that; he'd manage.

Though he needed a piss more than he ever had in his life right now. Should have gone before he left the pub, really, but again it would have meant barging through all those people.

There was an alley just opposite, he'd go in there. Might not hurt as much as last time, which had been like trying to pee razor blades. Might be okay – there might not be blood in it this time.

Gareth managed to get his coat on after several attempts. *Come on,* he reprimanded himself, *you can do it. Every journey begins with a first step.* He aimed for the alley, zig-zagging as he went. He thought he was doing okay until he reached the neck of it, when his legs went one way and his body the other. Gareth flung out his hands, snatching at thin air, and then scraping his fingers on the brick wall of the closest building. Rather than stabilizing him, this caused him to rebound like a pinball and strike the opposite wall. He fell heavily against it, recognising only a dull pain in his temple – the alcohol numbing most of it. Next thing he knew, he was on the floor, breathing heavily.

Gareth touched his forehead and was dully aware of his fingers coming away wet, though whether this was from the scraping they'd taken or the head wound was unclear. *Everything* was unclear at the moment. Apart from the building pressure in his bladder, which was still very apparent. Gareth sighed, attempting to get his feet underneath him again. It was a slow process, but he finally managed it, and he leaned against the wall for a moment, shoulder pressed up against the brickwork.

It was as he was about to turn, to fumble with his zip and release the stream of yellow liquid threatening to burst out of him, that he saw the figure down the alley some distance away. It was another blur at first, but Gareth heard the person too. Heard those disgusting sounds he was making, at any rate. The watery coughs, the awful retching. He stood there listening for a moment, wincing.

The figure was doubled over, and it sounded like they were spewing their guts up. Obviously someone who – unlike Gareth – couldn't handle their booze (yeah, and who just fell over in this self-same alleyway?). But Jesus, they really sounded like they were in trouble. Could he just carry on taking a piss while that was going on? Maybe they really needed help?

Gareth sighed again, and called out: "Hey... hey, are you all... all right down there?" His voice echoed off the walls, making it sound louder than he'd intended.

No answer, only more of the retching noises.

Gareth took an apprehensive step closer. "What washit?" he asked. "Too many Stellas or somethin'?"

The figure, illuminated by the streetlamps at the other end of the narrow lane, looked up. Just some youth, couldn't have been more than mid-twenties, Gareth thought – though his judgment wasn't exactly impeccable at the moment. The lad was sick again, this time dropping to his knees, then falling over on his back. Still using the wall for guidance, Gareth made his way along, getting closer and closer to the vomiting kid. He was only a few metres away now, near enough to see that the youth was choking, head back and neck thrust out, rasps replacing the retching sounds.

"Bloody hell," Gareth whispered, almost slipping again on the unsteady ground. "Ish okay, it'll be all right." Even as he was saying the words, he knew they held no conviction. Gareth didn't know first aid, and even if he had, wasn't in any fit state to perform it. The lad was convulsing, body jerking like ten thousand volts were coursing through it. Phone – he should call an ambulance, get some paramedics out here. Gareth put his hand in his jacket pocket; it was empty. So was the other one. Maybe he'd put his mobile in his trousers? Nope, wasn't there either. More than likely he'd left it back at the bed-sit, forgotten it again in his haste to be out, to get an early round in before things heated up. Well, they were certainly hotting up now, weren't they? If he didn't do something quick this guy—

The body stopped jerking, the youth lying there with bits of sick splattered all around his mouth. Gareth sucked in a breath through his teeth, then got down tentatively to shake him.

But, as he reached out, something peculiar happened. The body simply disappeared. Gareth blinked, frowned, and pulled back, hitting the wall again. *What the fuck?* He stared at the patch of ground where the kid had been twitching spasmodically only moments before, hand going to his mouth. "What... what the fuck?" he spluttered out loud this time, the words reverberating in the alley. Gareth looked left and right, perhaps to find a witness to this impossible event. Someone who'd tell him he wasn't going round the bend, that the lad had just been here but was fine now, had got up and run away before Gareth could—

No, there hadn't been the time for that. Okay, his senses weren't fantastic right now, but he knew when someone had been there one moment and—

He was hallucinating, that was it. A bad pint? *Too many* pints, more like – and spirits, come to that. Wasn't that one of the things he'd been warned about? Symptoms he might experience if he persevered with his favourite pastime?

Maybe it wasn't that at all. Maybe he'd struck his head harder than he'd thought? His vision was still blurred, but that was nothing unusual for Gareth. He was used to seeing everything in doubles and triples; used to ordering in those quantities as well.

The urgent need to urinate had deserted him, replaced temporarily by confusion. He should get out of there, get back to his place as soon as possible, retrieve that bottle he may have stashed somewhere and just have another drink (or several). He definitely needed one, more so now than ever. And wasn't it much darker than it had been a moment ago, the glow from the streetlamp not extending quite as far into the alley as he'd imagined?

Gareth chose the quickest way out: moving

forward rather than retreating. Even though it was only a single street's difference, he found himself disorientated. Thankfully there were people about, mainly emerging from clubs in the centre of town – the throbbing beat of which he could hear even at this distance. They were the kind of places he'd have expected the young lad to have come from: the one he'd seen... *thought* he'd seen... chucking up back there. Gareth had to remind himself that he hadn't really seen anything at all, it had just been his imagination.

A gaggle of young girls tottered past, skirts like belts – impossibly spiked high heels the only reason they could walk on the slippery ground so easily. They were laughing and joking with each other, raucous laughter piercing the night air. One – with backcombed hair like the Bride of Frankenstein – glanced sideways at Gareth, who was gaping across at her. "What you lookin' at, you old pervo?" she mouthed off, her speech just as affected as his. She took a swig from the bottle she held, pulled a face at him when he didn't answer, and continued to laugh and joke with the group.

And then they were gone, but as Gareth looked again he saw they'd left a member of their group behind. A blonde-haired girl was sitting on the edge of the pavement, as if she couldn't go on any further. Like the others, she had an extremely short skirt – black leather rolled up over thighs that looked like chopped liver, all red and mottled. Her leopard-skin vest was even thinner, providing no protection from the cold. And Gareth saw the evidence of that when she blew out a long breath of steam, emerging from pouty red lips like smoke from a volcano.

Maybe she's just having a rest? he thought. Resting feet that she'd crammed inside those designer torture devices.

Her heavily-mascaraed eyes were almost slits, and she was lolling over strangely to one side. Then she dropped over completely, embracing the pavement like it was a soft mattress, kicking out her legs so they were half on the path, half on the road. She was going to sleep, right there in the middle of the street. So tired and drunk she was going to make it her bed for the night. She'd die of exposure, dressed like that!

Gareth thought about Sara, and how in a few years' time she might be out clubbing with girls like this herself. This was someone's daughter, and if she were his child, he'd expect a passer-by to help her. At least cover her up or something until they could—

He was already heading across the road before he had time to stop himself, shrugging off his coat. Gareth paused when he reached her, not only because of how this might look to those who happened by ("What you doin', you old pervo? Tryin' to cop a feel, eh?") but also because of the bizarre appearance of the girl in question. Like the lad back in the alleyway, the one who'd been throwing up, she too was... well, she was glowing. The streetlamp was definitely quite a distance away from her, yet she was lit up like – *go on, say it* – like a Christmas tree. It was an unnatural light, and yet it seemed the most natural thing in the universe. Like sun or moonlight.

Gareth dawdled, holding his coat in both hands as if he was fighting a bull. The girl was snoring softly, more proof that she was asleep. Then she simply stopped. Stopped snoring; stopped *breathing*. He snapped himself out of his stupor, dropping his coat and kneeling on the pavement next to her. Beneath the tons of make-up he saw at this close range the face of an innocent teenager, a girl who'd barely had time to live at all. And, if he didn't do something about it, never would.

He cocked his head, listening more closely for any sign of air, of her lungs working. *Pulse*, he thought through the thick treacle of his mind, *I should feel for a pulse – sod what it looks like.*

"Lost summin' down there?" asked a voice, and Gareth looked up. Standing there was a man in a low-cut white T-shirt that almost looked like a blouse.

Gareth shook his head, pointing to the girl. "She'sh... I think she'sh shtopped... she'sh not breathing." He had difficulty with the complex sentence, but felt sure he'd communicated his meaning well enough that this man might help, phone an ambulance where Gareth could not. Just like he'd needed someone to with the lad back in that alley, the one who'd—

Gareth followed the puzzled man's gaze, down to the empty pavement beneath him. The girl had vanished. "Who is?" asked the blouse-guy, giving a little laugh. "You're seeing things, mate. Well gone, aren't you? Look, why don't you let me get you into a cab?" He reached out for Gareth's arm, but it was yanked away. Not because he didn't want to go with the man, but more because he needed to stay, needed to assure himself that the girl had actually *been* here – asleep on the pavement. Curled up, freezing to death.

"Suit yourself," snapped the guy, walking off and leaving Gareth to it. "They wouldn't have taken you anyway," he called over his shoulder. The man was probably right; no taxi driver in his right mind would have given Gareth a lift, even if he'd wanted one now. Even if he'd changed his mind about the expense.

Gareth sat on the pavement where the girl had been curled up only moments ago, shaking his head. A head that was starting to throb, not with the relentless bass blaring out from the nightclubs, but with its own internal rhythm. He felt a stab of pain as well, at the temple.

God, he needed that drink!

Get up, he told himself. *Get up and get yourself home – just start walking, it won't take you long. Then you can have one. Think about the way it'll slide down your throat, filling you up with that warmth that'll spread throughout your body.*

As opposed to the coldness he felt, a chill that was starting to sober him up; something he'd never been a big fan of. Gareth reached around on the pavement for his coat, finally snatching it up and gratefully tugging his arms into it again. He turned over, attempting to scramble to his feet.

Gareth heard the sound of the car before he saw it, snapping his head to the side quickly enough to launch himself out of its way. Gareth rolled unceremoniously over onto the pavement just as the thing scraped the curb. It was weaving erratically as it sped away from the scene, leaving Gareth gaping at what had just happened.

"Fuck me! You – you bloody lunatic!" he shouted after the vehicle, a dingy red saloon that was now threatening to veer onto the wrong side of the road. What the hell was happening tonight? *Just what the bloody hell?*

As he began to get up again, swaying a little from side to side, he heard the screaming. It was coming from the direction the car had headed off in, taking the corner at speed and with very little finesse. Part of him just wanted to walk away, not get involved with more of this madness. It wasn't his... wasn't his *responsibility*. Just like the girl, Sara – no, *not* Sara – and the lad back in the alley hadn't been, either. That's what you got for trying to be a good Samaritan. Your mind screwed with you, apparently.

But the screams grew louder, and he just had to see.

There were other people not far away, more revellers wandering the streets. They appeared not to have heard the cries, which were still going on, still so shrill they should have woken the dead. Gareth thought about calling to them, but what was the use? They were obviously too drunk or high to notice. He wished he was in that state himself, instead of sobering up – he was at the halfway house between Slaughteredfield and Sobrietyville. Wished he was drunk anyway; he'd never touched drugs. Never needed to, the liquor gave him everything he could ever want.

Waving his hand, dismissing them – not that they'd notice – he went off in search of the source of the wailing, absently remembering to look both ways before crossing back over the road.

When he turned the corner himself, he saw what the commotion was. It was a scene right out of a soap opera. On the side of the road lay a woman, dressed a lot more sensibly than the girls he'd seen earlier: a long coat over trousers and boots. Perhaps it was because she was more mature – in her thirties Gareth guessed, late thirties maybe, with short, straight hair. One of those trousered legs was sticking out at an odd angle, though, obviously broken. She was also clutching at her side, sitting awkwardly. None of this was the cause of her screaming, however. In the middle of the road was another person, this one face down, crumpled and lying in a pool of what could only be his own blood (the closer Gareth dared to inch, the more he could work out that it *was* a he, perhaps the woman's partner?).

The car that had almost hit Gareth wasn't that far away, either. It had run into a lamppost, practically wrapping itself around it. The post itself, though cracked, had barely buckled – the light was flickering on and off, however. Yet the whole tableau seemed perfectly lit, Gareth noted, as if a camera crew had been filming it for that primetime television audience. A Christmas soap *special* in fact, which people would watch and comment: "My life may be shit, but at least it's not as bad as theirs!"

Not as bad in the slightest. How could *anything* be as bad as this? Gareth couldn't imagine. He found himself drawing ever nearer to the devastation, his heart going out to the felled woman, the tears streaming down her face as she just gazed at the prone form of the man, shrieking her disbelief – barely noticing Gareth's presence.

It was pretty plain what had happened. The 'bloody lunatic', as Gareth had labelled the driver, had slammed into this couple. Either they'd been crossing the road, or walking on the pavement, but that didn't matter to the psycho-driver. The car had struck the man and thrown him up into the air, to land, almost certainly dead, on the tarmac. The woman had been clipped and sent spinning sideways, parted from her companion in more ways than one. The car had only stopped when it had to, when the lamppost had *forced* it to. A something object meeting a something else... Gareth had learnt that at school, though it had been many years and many, many obliterated brain cells ago.

He picked his way across to the woman. "Look, just wait there. I'll..." The sentence got away from him. He was going to do what, exactly? Phone the emergency services on his non-existent mobile? And where exactly was she going to go anyway, with that smashed leg? Smashed side as well, Gareth saw, redness pumping its way through the coat and her fingers. What a fucking mess.

He hadn't seen the half of it yet, though – hadn't seen the interior of the car, which he finally made his way towards, curiosity again getting the better of him. Now that *was* a mess. There were two of them inside, not much older than the girl sleeping on the pavement – both male this time, however. The driver had been catapulted through the windscreen, or at least his front half had. His head and shoulders were poking through the shattered glass, midriff bent over the steering wheel. His passenger was lolling back in the seat, head at an impossible slant, neck almost definitely broken. His tongue was lolling too, out of his mouth and to the side. His glassy eyes stared out at Gareth, seeing nothing.

There was blood everywhere.

Gareth withdrew, returning to the woman – who was slumped over on the floor. There were no screams now, no noise at all. She hadn't had to wait long, it seemed, before joining her loved one, wherever he was, in death. Gareth bit his lip, screwed up his eyes.

When I look again, this will all be gone, he told himself. *Just like the others. This isn't really happening, I'm not seeing this.*

Gareth opened his eyes again and the scene was still there. The bodies, the wrecked car. He frowned. Maybe this really had happened, and like the boy who cried wolf he hadn't believed it the third time – when it had actually been real. But that would mean...

Just as he was about to shout for help – try to get someone's attention, *make* them come over and see what he'd seen – the scene rippled, shifted, and then evaporated. As solid as it had all looked just a second ago, now there was nothing. Even the streetlamp was working fine, standing tall and straight, no damage at all.

He was going crazy, he had to be. No: crazy people don't realise that they're crazy. They think they're sane. The very fact he was thinking that meant he was okay. Didn't it?

Gareth wiped a shaky hand over his face. *Okay?* How could *any* of this be okay? It wasn't even close!

He staggered away from the area, from any kind of reminders about what he'd just observed, what he'd just been shown. But that wasn't the end of it. No matter where he went, there were more sights, more things to see:

On one corner he saw a fight break out between two men, their blows sloppy but vicious. In the end one of them took out a knife and stabbed the other, who simultaneously managed to get a lucky punch in. That sent the second man reeling into a closed shop front. Neither of them moved as Gareth looked on, as he watched the scene fade, just as the others had before.

In another shop doorway, he saw a homeless person wrapped in rags, hair grey, straggly and unkempt, face dirty. He was clutching what remained of a bottle of clear liquid, cradling it in his arms like a baby. He'd also wet himself. Gareth stared, transfixed. *Is this a vision of my future?* he wondered. Was it going to come to this? With slow movements, the tramp drained what was left of his drink, settled back on the steps and leaned his head on the side of the door jamb. Then he stopped moving; there was no longer steam coming from his mouth. And, moments later, he was gone, as if he'd never existed at all.

Then, somehow, Gareth found he'd ended up near the river. The surface was partly frozen over, and someone had thought it was a brilliant idea to go walking across the thin ice. He thought about calling out to warn them, but knew there was no use. So Gareth simply stood and watched as it cracked and the person fell through into freezing cold water. Two arms flailed about, drowning cries echoing through the night. Next thing, there was nothing: no noise, no movement. Not even a hole any more.

Gareth saw drunk people playing chicken at train crossings and losing to 150 tons of metal travelling at ridiculous speeds – that was even more messy than the car crash, but at least it was mercifully quick; he saw people climbing up scaffolding, thinking they were superheroes – unaware of the great danger they were in, lacking the skill and dexterity needed to stay on the side of those buildings – falling from various heights like lemmings from a cliff; he saw deaths of every conceivable kind, as if the city itself had recorded them and was now hitting playback, the echoes of so many lives lost. Needlessly so: that was the tragedy of it.

All of these incidents had two things in common. First, the same tinge to them those first few had had – that *glow* about them, natural yet unnatural. It was how Gareth had come to differentiate the real from the unreal.

They were also drink-related. All of these people, all these – *go on, admit it* – ghosts, shades, *spirits*, whatever you wanted to call them, so many now they were surrounding him, causing Gareth's vision to swim and his head to spin (though ironically, he was growing more sober by the minute), would all be alive today were it not for the thing he held most dear. The thing that had taken over his life. His love, his obsession, his everything.

Gareth spun with the visions, twirling and whirling until he thought he would throw up himself – just like that first lad he'd seen back in the alley, how long ago now? He had no idea. Felt like several lifetimes.

"Leave me alone, please!" he shouted. "What do you want from me, for Chrissake!"

He spun and spun, until he could take it no more. Everything glowed now, the figures merging – and it was so bright he thought he'd go blind. Except no oblivion followed, only more illumination. *Moving* light: going across, back and forth.

Left and right, right to left. And Gareth followed it with his eyes.

"Okay, there doesn't appear to be any sign of concussion," he heard a voice say. A female voice. Gareth blinked: once, twice. The light was gone now, as quickly as some of those scenes had vanished. Gone with a click, a thumb pressing a button.

To be replaced with a face, looming over him. A woman with kindly features, hair gathered up in a bun. He blinked again, taking in her blue scrubs. "Are... are you real?" he asked.

She smiled. "Last time I checked."

It was noisy where he was, lots of chatter, the odd raised voice. "Where...?" He didn't finish the sentence, but didn't really need to.

"You're in the Casualty department, Mr..." He saw the woman look up and over at a nurse. "Mr Powell. I'm Dr Roberts. You were found wandering around, a little bit the worse for wear. Had too much to drink, though I'm sure this isn't the first time judging from the colour of your skin."

"I saw..." Gareth shook his head, unable to

explain. He couldn't even explain it to himself, let alone anyone else. "I hit my head, didn't I?"

Dr Roberts nodded. "Yes. It's just grazed though, fortunately. Same goes for your fingers." She nodded at the plasters covering his fingertips. "Could have been a lot worse."

It was Gareth's turn to nod. He knew, he'd seen what 'a lot worse' looked like. Seen too much of that.

"Oh, and we had to get you out of your trousers. You'd... well..." Gareth frowned, then realised that the impetus for heading into that alley in the first place must have returned – probably when it had all got too much for him. Pissed himself, like some kind of animal. Like—

He suddenly remembered the tramp: *Is this a vision of my future?*

Someone tapped the doctor on the shoulder, and she turned. "You'll have to excuse me, Mr Powell. Busy time of year, Christmas. Too many people making merry and all that."

I can well imagine, thought Gareth. But was that all it had been, he wondered, his imagination? The knock on the head hadn't been that serious, but maybe that combined with the drink? It had all seemed so real...

He looked over to where the doctor had gone. A stretcher had just been wheeled in, paramedics pumping air into a young lad not dissimilar to the one who'd choked on his own vomit. He heard one of the ambulance crew say something about alcohol poisoning. The doctor pulled back the kid's eyelids, checking *his* pupils now. Then a nurse pulled the curtain shut, blocking off Gareth's view.

It was a good while before Dr Roberts returned, time which Gareth had used to think. He felt clearer than he had in such a long time; it was a start at least. His recent memories were anything but fleeting – indeed, he doubted he'd *ever* forget them.

When the curtain was pulled back again and the doctor stepped in, Gareth asked her how the boy was. "He'll pull through, I think," she replied, "this time, at least. Why?"

"He just reminds me of someone, that's all," Gareth said, hoarsely.

"I see... Now, about your situation—" Roberts began, but Gareth held up a hand to stop her.

"I know what you're going to say, and you're right." He swallowed dryly; had a feeling he'd be doing a lot of that in the months to come, if it wasn't too late for him already. Gareth nodded to himself, as if deciding finally. He *was* an animal, a creature of habit, but it was time to break that habit. Time to actually get things under control instead of pretending, kidding himself. "I – I need help, Doctor. I realise that now. I need help to quit."

She smiled again. "I was going to say, we'll give you a scan just to make sure about..." Dr Roberts tapped her head. "But I'm *very* happy to hear you say that, especially on a night like tonight. When you've seen some of the things drink can do to people—"

"Oh, I have," Gareth cut in. "Trust me, I've seen it all."

"Right then," said the doctor, still smiling. "And here was I thinking Christmas miracles didn't happen anymore."

Gareth smiled back. He used to hate this time of year, but perhaps he'd been wrong. Perhaps he'd been wrong about a great many things. He had a mental flash of the frozen young girl then, and thought about his daughter. Yes, definitely wrong about a lot of things. About Sara being better off without...

It would be a long – and probably slippery –

road, but the alternative didn't bear thinking about. *Come on*, he told himself. *You can do it.*

And now that the first step had been taken, he felt certain those ghosts, those *spirits* of Christmas, had got what they wanted. That they would be resting a little easier tonight.

Gareth hoped so, at any rate.

Marlowe's Ghost

Maybe it was his imagination, or the fact he'd just pulled a four hour shift at the refuge – doling out food and a kindly word to those less fortunate than himself – but he was pretty sure when he came to open the front door of his block of flats, the list of names on the column of buzzers beside him turned into a face.

The names of the tenants in this ramshackle building, the words themselves, had slipped from their perches on their respective lines and begun to form a pattern. The buttons joined in, turning themselves into nostrils, a pair of eyes, a mouth. A mouth which spoke his name even as he was putting his key into the lock.

A mouth belonging to a face he knew all too

well. The face of his best friend who'd died several years ago now, stabbed to death on a street corner for the money he'd been carrying.

"Eric," said the mouth, forming the name with those buttons, the jumbled words making creases in this strange face. "Eric..." The voice was almost a whisper, causing him to bend down and cock an ear.

"Jared?"

He stared at the sight of his long-dead friend, now rendered in ink and plastic. Then he blinked twice, and when he did the list of names and their corresponding buttons returned to normal.

Eric shook his head and stared at the list once more, daring it to change again. Daring *something* to happen. But it didn't. He sighed, hefted the brown paper bag he was carrying, turned the key in the lock, and entered the building.

The first thing that greeted him was the stink; not of one thing in particular, just the accumulated aroma of the kind of people who lived here. It smelt like despair. He made his way to the lift, past graffiti on the stained walls proclaiming everything from 'Carol Luvz Tony' to 'For a Good Time Ring...' complete with mobile number. He jabbed at the button and waited for the lift to come. Nothing happened. The blessed thing was broken yet again, and the chances of anyone coming out to see to it this late on Christmas Eve were slim to negligible.

Sighing again, Eric made his way to the stairs, ready to climb the thirteen floors to his small flat. On the way, he had to walk past a gang of youths who were quite blatantly dealing drugs. He kept his head down and left them to it – it was the best way to avoid getting a kicking, he'd found. Eric also had to negotiate a section of stairway which was in total darkness – the lights above having been smashed a couple of weeks ago (again, there was no sign that anyone was coming out to fix them in a hurry).

As Eric wearily climbed the steps, he thought again about the face. It was hardly surprising, the more he dwelled on it. For one thing he was shattered – even before the refuge, he'd worked a full day at the office, catching up with work that had been piled on his desk by his boss, Mr Fitzgerald, so the man could take a long break over the holidays. Not that Eric minded: it was good, steady work, even if he did only get paid a pittance to virtually run that office.

Then there was the timing of the 'vision'. The anniversary of Jared Marlowe's murder. Of course the man would be on his mind, because while everyone else was celebrating there was still a part of Eric that was in mourning for the best mate he'd ever had in his life. The man he'd worked alongside, who'd inspired him to get into the whole charity scene in the first place. You could never hope to meet a more kindly, generous soul than Jared; taken well before his time.

Eric reached the front door of his flat, and was about to insert another key to let himself in when he noticed the lock had been busted. Hanging his head, he nudged the door open with trembling fingers, aware that whoever had broken in might still be around (and was also probably one of his neighbours, looking for things they could sell to get high – possibly even some of the guys he'd seen on the stairs). Eric snapped on the light, readying himself, though he had no idea what he'd be able to do if he caught them in the act.

Fortunately, there was no-one inside anymore. His small bed-sit had been turned over all right – his chairs tipped up, sofa-bed in disarray, his bare Christmas tree kicked across the room – but the culprits had left empty-handed, mainly because there hadn't been anything in there to steal. Kitchen cupboards had been flung open, but what little food he had for the Xmas period he was carrying under his arm right now. Eric didn't own any electrical items like a TV, stereo or a DVD player. He didn't have that much free time to watch shows or movies – preferring instead, when he could, to kick back with a good—

Dropping his bag on the floor, he ran to the shelves where he kept the books he read at night. The well-thumbed paperbacks were still there, if strewn all over the place, but what had been taken were the leather-bound editions of classics his sister had given him all those years ago.

If Eric had been a swearing man, he would have done so right then. As it was he settled for a very strong "Bugger!"

He thought about ringing the police but A) He didn't have a phone, mobile or otherwise, and B) the police weren't likely to do much about it anyway. He'd heard many of the residents complaining about thefts and not one of them, to his knowledge, had ever gotten any joy from chasing things up...or indeed got their belongings back. Eric supposed he should be grateful he didn't have that much to steal, but the books had meant a great deal to him. The only real reminders of Faye he had.

You still have a living reminder, he told himself, *in the form of Fraser, her only son.* He'd heard from the young man only that afternoon, seeing if his uncle wanted to get together for a drink over Christmas.

"You know I don't drink, Fraser," Eric had told him, keeping his voice low as he wasn't supposed to take personal calls at work. "I've seen too much of what it can do to people on the streets."

"God, you really need to chillax, Unc," Fraser had told him. "Have a few laughs."

Going out and getting wasted wasn't the kind of thing that brought Eric pleasure. His work at the refuge, and tomorrow down at the soup kitchen – not to mention the charity fun run he was doing on Boxing Day – those were the kinds of things that brought him joy.

But Fraser was just Fraser, a whizz-kid computer expert with money to burn and the hedonistic lifestyle to match. Many's the time

Eric had tried to get him to donate to some of the worthy causes he was involved in, but Fraser always told him he could put his cash to better use. It made Eric sad.

Though not as sad as the loss of those books. He sighed again, knowing nothing could be done and that he really should get some sleep before his early start the next morning. Eric touched the shelf where the tomes had once rested, then turned and retrieved his bag, taking it into the kitchen and unloading it. Inside was a pack of processed turkey slices, a few potatoes and some other vegetables: his Christmas dinner. He stowed them away in his larder (Eric didn't bother with a fridge as it was so cold inside the flat – especially at this time of year – that food was unlikely to spoil). The bread and cheese he left out as a snack before bedtime as he hadn't eaten since his usual lunch in the canteen.

Next he set to work trying to fix the door lock, tying string around the handle in an effort to make do for the night. Not the most secure of barriers, but what other choice did he have? He righted one of his chairs, then sat and looked at the door as he ate his bread and cheese – drinking a glass of water from the tap.

The meter ran out before he was quite ready for bed, so he had to light a couple of candles. They provided not only illumination, but a bit of heat as well. He picked up his Christmas tree, such as it was, and pulled out the sofa-bed, getting under the covers with his clothes still on.

In spite of everything that had happened – Jared and the break-in – Eric still felt happy when he thought of the good he'd done tonight, and all he *would* do over the next couple of days while he was off work (all the time Fitzgerald would allow him). It left a glow inside him as warm as those from the candles, and it wasn't long before his eyelids began to droop.

~

It was a rumbling sound that made them snap open again. At first he thought it might be his stomach, as that often made strange sounds at night, especially if he hadn't had enough to eat. But no. This was outside his door, something – or some*one* – making their way towards it. Eric sat up on the sofa-bed, the noise growing louder: a heavy thudding now, like boots on the floorboards.

The burglars, he thought, *they've come back!*

Eric pulled up the covers, staring at the front

door in the light from the waning candles. He jumped when the first bang came, thudding against the door's surface so hard it rattled the hinges. That was followed by another, then another, each one louder than the last.

"Go... Go away," Eric managed, finding his voice, but only just. It sounded like a mouse trying to shoo away a lion. "There's nothing left. You've taken everything I have."

There was another thud on the door, this one threatening to splinter the wood like Jack Nicholson on an axe-wielding spree.

What do they want? There was no way he was going to let them in.

Thud! Thud!

"Look, just go away!" Eric repeated, his voice rising a bit higher; it was the best he could muster in the circumstances.

They didn't go away, though. Instead the people outside his door seemed to redouble their efforts, slamming harder on it until the string holding the knob began to unravel. Eric leaned back on his bed, pulling the covers up. If they got in here, he didn't stand a chance. He was a wiry individual, but not built for fighting: he had neither the frame nor the stomach for it. They'd pulverise him. Maybe even do to him what they did to—

Jared.

Eric stared, open-mouthed, at the doorway. The door itself had been knocked down, landing with a bump and sending dust flying in every direction. In its place stood a lone figure, rather than the gang he'd imagined. Its shape was indistinct, made worse by the flickering of the candles, but in spite of this Eric was able to make out its face quite clearly. It was the face he'd seen downstairs at the front door, the face of the man he'd had to identify in the morgue after the stabbing.

"Jared?" he said out loud.

"Hiya Eric, how's things?" asked his former best friend as he made his way further into the bed-sit.

As he'd done before, Eric blinked, only this time the image didn't go away. *I must be asleep*, he thought. That was it; he'd been drifting off when the banging noise started. It was some kind of nightmare brought on from seeing what he thought he'd seen as he'd been turning the front door key. That being the case, he saw no harm in replying.

"Things are… They're… I'm…" He completely lost the thread of what he was saying. "How have you been keeping, yourself?"

"How have I been…?" Jared laughed; it was a hollow sound. Then he didn't so much walk into the room, as float. "How does it bloody well look like I've been keeping?"

Eric screwed up his eyes this time, but all that did was bring the rest of Jared into sharper focus. Now he could see the man's tatty suit and raincoat – it was the one he'd been wearing the evening of the attack – and he could see the red stains where the knife had slid into him, at the chest and torso. Jared touched one of the wounds and his fingers came away crimson.

"I'm dead, Eric. It isn't a whole lot of fun, I can tell you. Now, I know exactly what you're thinking, mate," said Jared, "but you're not dreaming this. It's real. I'm here. That was me before with the buzzers, too. Neat trick, eh?"

Eric looked past Jared, wondering why his neighbours hadn't reacted to the ruckus, come out to at least see what was happening. Perhaps they'd decided they didn't want to get involved.

"Don't worry about them, they can't hear me. It's you I've come to talk to." Jared smiled, but it was a chilling sight – his face was blue-white, his teeth stained where he'd coughed up blood.

"It's the cheese, then," murmured Eric. If he wasn't asleep, it had to be what he'd eaten before bed.

"What's that? Cheese? Hardly. Since when was cheese used to call forth ghosts from beyond the veil?"

"I meant it had affected me," explained Eric. "Poisoned me somehow."

"Oh," said Jared, "I see. No, it's not down to any kind of dairy products, I'm afraid. I wish it was that simple." Jared frowned, then pulled up the chair Eric had been sitting on, keeping vigil at the door. He looked around at the flat. "So, this is where you've ended up. Onwards and upwards, eh? The place I was in when I was alive looked like a palace compared to this, and that's saying something."

Eric tentatively leaned forward on the sofa-bed. "And where..." He swallowed dryly. "Where did *you* end up?"

"I'd have thought that was bloody well obvious."

Eric shook his head. It wasn't to him.

"All right," said Jared, also leaning forwards. "Now listen. What I'm going to tell you, what I've come here to say tonight before it's too late... it might not go down very well with you."

"I don't understand," said Eric.

"No, and that's the whole thing. You really don't understand how things work. How could you? You're still... Well, you're still *alive*, not to put too fine a point on it." Jared looked him in right in the eye. "But that's a good thing. Much better than the alternative, I can tell you. It's just what you're doing with the time you've got left that's the problem."

Eric still wasn't following him.

"All right," Jared clapped his hands together. "Where to begin? Okay, you remember what I used to be like in life, don't you?"

Eric nodded. Of course he did, he'd just been thinking about it tonight, when all this happened (which gave even more credence to the notion that he was either dreaming or whacked out on dodgy stilton).

"Always giving, always doing something for someone. Working my fingers to the bone to earn money to give away. Mankind was my business, Eric. Just like it's yours now."

Eric gave another nod. "You were the one who taught me that."

"Not intentionally, I have to add. But, well, let me teach you another lesson, before you have to learn it the hard way, my friend." There was a bitterness to Jared's voice which hadn't been there when Eric had known him. Then again, maybe that's what being stabbed to death did to you. "Everything I ever did, all the people I helped, and what did it get me? I was knobbled taking the charity money we'd raised standing on freezing street corners to the bank."

Eric's eyes fell. "I know. And I'm sorry. Maybe if I'd gone with you—"

"Then you'd be just as dead as me, mate. Don't you get it? Regardless of everything we did, no-one had our back."

"What do you mean?"

"I mean I could have been cut some slack, you know? You fight the good fight, then you expect a few favours along the way."

Eric saw what he was getting at now, and was very surprised to hear it. "That isn't how it works."

"Fucking tell me about it," spat Jared, taking Eric aback again, especially with his bad language.

"That wasn't why we did what we did."

Jared leaned even further forwards, wagging his finger. "Maybe not, but perhaps, when I tell you this, you might see things a little differently."

Eric doubted he would. He wasn't the person he was because he wanted something in return, even if it was protection against the horrors of the world. What happened to Jared had a certain kind of warped irony to it, but that didn't mean he should have expected to be saved that night, no matter how much he or Eric wanted it.

"No-one intervened because nobody was there to, mate. I didn't go on to get any stars in my crown because there's nothing... afterwards. Nothing at all."

"What?" gasped Eric.

"Why do you think I'm still hanging around here instead of there? Why do you think I still look like this? I'm stuck in the form I had when I died. Took me all this time to even appear corporeally. It's a lot harder than all those films make it look. And as for Clarence and his mob..." He swivelled on the seat. "Do you see any wings? Well, do ya? No, didn't think so."

"Maybe you're working for the other side, then?" Eric ventured.

"There *are* no sides! That's what I've been

trying to tell you." Jared looked genuinely hurt by this, and Eric did feel guilty for thinking it. Jared had done a lot of good in his time, more so even than him. Would he really have gone over to the dark side? "Look, believe what you like, but I'm telling you there's blackness, Eric. You die and there's nothing. No white light. No warm fuzzy feeling. No gates. Nada."

Eric thought for a moment about this. If Jared *was* right, then that would alter a fair few people's opinions about how to conduct themselves in *this* world. But that didn't include him. Eric wasn't doing what he was doing for any kind of reward, in this world or the next.

"I thought you might feel that way," Jared told him, reading his thoughts again. "That's why I brought a little back-up. I don't want you wasting what's left of your life, like I did mine. Now that *really* would be a sin."

"I'm not wasting—"

Jared held up his bloodied hand. "Shut up, Eric. Whether you like it or not, you're going to be visited by three ghosts... and Derek Acorah." Jared grinned when he saw the terrified look on Eric's face. "All right, I was only joking about him. I wouldn't wish that on anyone. But you are going to meet three of my lot: those who make it their business to show mortals the truth – before it's too late."

"Then I'll refuse to see them."

"Expect the first at 1 o'clock," said Jared, ignoring him and getting up.

"Wait a second," Eric said, rising too. "How will I know him?"

Jared, who was fading out even as he began walking away from Eric, looked over his shoulder and, grinning again, said: "He'll be wearing a pink carnation."

Then the spectre of Eric's late best friend vanished from sight – leaving the room the way it had been before he appeared (door and string intact), and leaving Eric wondering if the encounter had even happened at all.

~

The First of the Three Spirits

Eric spent the next thirty minutes or so looking at his watch, hoping either it had all been a hallucination or he was still snoring away to himself on the sofa-bed rather than checking the time.

When 1 o'clock came and went, he breathed a huge sigh of relief. Regardless of whether he was awake or asleep, the ghost Jared had talked about hadn't shown up.

No sooner had he thought this than the room began to shake. Eric tapped his watch. "Bugger," he said, remembering now that he always set it fast so he'd never be late for anything. Eric held onto the bed as it rattled beneath him, a terrible wind building up, swirling around and putting out the candles – yet the room was still well lit, swelling with a preternatural glow. Eric felt a presence behind him, and turned to see a figure standing in his kitchen. It was sepia in colour, and from certain angles looked to be an old man, but from others it had the face of a young boy – even a baby.

"Hello Eric," said the apparition in a shrill voice.

"W-W-Who are you?" spluttered Eric, his teeth chattering at the sight.

The thing floated through into what Eric laughably called his living room, tutting. As it did so, Eric saw that its body was made up of old photographs, layered on top of one another. "Show a little backbone, man! It's no wonder Angela did what she did."

Angela. Eric hadn't thought about her in so long. Now, thanks to this... thing he saw her face again, saw her as she *used* to be. He shut his eyes, shaking his head. "That's what you're trying to do, isn't it? To change my mind? Make me think about the past?"

"Well, I wasn't going to, but what a great idea!" said the ghost. It took a photo from its chest and threw it at Eric. "Here, take a look at this."

Eric couldn't help himself. He picked up the old photo and stared at it, recognising a twelve-year-old him, outside, playing in the snow with a bunch of other kids: hiding behind cars and lampposts, throwing snowballs at each other, at passers-by. One old woman shuddered when a cold projectile struck her back and the young Eric giggled.

"At least you knew how to have fun back then," the ghost said to him, and Eric suddenly realised they were actually *in* the photograph, the edges still clearly defined.

Eric stood transfixed, watching his younger self. He'd forgotten all about this, about the Christmases he'd spent playing with pals from school.

"Eric! Eric? Where are you? It's time for tea!

It's your favourite, chips, fish-fingers and mushy peas."

He recognised his mother's voice immediately, turning to look for her even as the young Eric started to snigger with his friends and ran off down the road.

"Where's he... Where am *I* going?" he asked, setting off after the boys. But the ghost held him back, shaking its head. "They can't see or hear us. How can they, when this is just a snapshot from long ago?"

But there was more to this 'snapshot', much more. Eric wanted to go back and see his mother, the woman who'd single-handedly brought up both him and his sister. But the ghost had other ideas.

"Not that way – up here," it said, pointing.

And suddenly they'd caught up with the younger Eric. He was hassling some other kid who was wearing glasses, down one of the alleyways. "I lent you that comic for four days, Baker. You've had it over a week now, where is it?"

"It's at home. I'm sorry. I keep forgetting to bring it back to school," answered the other kid, obviously frightened.

Eric couldn't remember any of this, or perhaps he'd blocked it out of his memory? But why? He soon saw when the younger *him* spoke again.

"Four days, fifty pence a day we said. That means you now owe me four quid, plus interest."

The kid with the glasses just gaped at him. "What?"

"You heard me," said the young Eric. "Pay up!"

"But... but I haven't got it. After Christmas I might have a little money but—"

"Not good enough," snapped Eric. "A deal's a deal and we shook on it. Alan, Sam." The younger Eric stepped aside and let his mates come forward. What the present day Eric saw next made him balk. His friends started to beat up the kid with glasses who couldn't pay.

"No, stop!" shouted the older Eric, moving forward again; then he remembered what the ghost had said. He couldn't affect things here because they'd already happened. The beating had already played itself out: at *his* behest. Eric watched his younger self enjoying the spectacle. How could he have been so cold?

"Pretty good little racket you had going, I'd say," the ghost told him. "Pity you didn't keep it up. You had a bit of an edge back then."

"No, I... this can't be right," said Eric.

"Oh, I assure you it is. You were always the troublemaker growing up, Eric. Your mum and Faye were constantly getting you out of scrapes. Don't you remember? Must have been something to do with not having a father figure."

Eric covered his face with his hands, but the ghost pulled them down, simultaneously handing him another photo from its body. Eric took it reluctantly, and felt compelled again to look at the scene: this time a nightclub with flashing lights and disco music. He frowned, then saw himself at the bar with a pint of lager. He was in his late teens maybe, still hanging around with a couple of mates, having a laugh, getting increasingly drunk.

(*You know I don't drink, Fraser. I've seen too much of what it can do to people.*)

Eric turned to the ghost, who was at the side of him again – this time jiving to the music. "*Yeah*, this is more like it," the thing that was both old and young at the same time, said. "Can't beat the '80s for dance tracks, can you?"

Eric ignored him, focussing instead on his younger self. He was being egged on by his pals to approach a young woman with blonde hair, who was also with a couple of friends. The trio of women kept turning around and pointing: laughing. Then the blonde one turned and looked at him.

"Angela," whispered the present-day Eric.

The ghost stopped dancing for a second and nodded. "Bit of all right, isn't she?"

She was more than that – she was stunning. Eric watched as his teenage self plucked up the courage to swagger across to her. All false bravado, he stumbled over a few corny chat-up lines which Angela's companions laughed at, then just asked if they wanted a drink. If *Angela* wanted a drink. He could see the hesitation in her eyes, but she nodded.

"Rum and coke," she told him.

Then later they'd danced, and he'd somehow persuaded her to give him a kiss under the mistletoe hanging from the glitter ball above the dance floor.

"So, one thing led to another and..." the ghost began. "What am I telling you for, you already know this story."

Eric did, but strangely enough he'd forgotten *how* exactly they'd met and how it had gone from there. It hurt too much to think about Angela at all these days.

The ghost danced around him, peeling off another photo – from its leg this time – and placed it in front of his nose. Here, Eric and Angela were in a flat, not that much bigger than the one he was in at the moment, but much more homely. Decorations were up, the tree was covered in tinsel and lights. Angela turned towards him and the ghost, the slight swelling of her pregnant belly clearly visible.

"Don't," said Eric, tears welling in his eyes. "Please don't show me this."

The ghost ignored him and let the scene unfold. Young Eric and Angela were talking about a job opportunity that he should take. After all, they were going to be a *proper* family soon.

"Mr Fitzgerald really seems like someone I could learn from," Eric was saying as he came up behind Angela, placing his arms around her and stroking her stomach.

"You should go for it," Angela told him. "Work your way up and in a few years, who knows where you'll be in the company?"

"But we both know where you ended up, don't we?" said the ghost, switching again between young and old. "You didn't learn from Fitzgerald at all. You learned instead from…"

Another photo, ripped from the ghost's arm, was shoved in front of Eric. It was of him and Jared meeting in the office. God, they both looked *soooo* young. Jared had clapped his hand, the grip firm. Here was a good man – unlike Fitzgerald, as Eric had discovered, with his underhand dealings and dodgy book-keeping. The more time Eric spent with Jared, the more he realised he could actually do something with his life. The amount of money Jared raised for various charities was something to aspire to, the amount of his time he set aside to spend with the poor, the needy, the sick.

It opened Eric's eyes. And once that had happened, they couldn't be closed again.

"But at what cost?" asked the ghost.

A further photo now, which Eric refused to even acknowledge – so the ghost forced him to see, sucking them both inside the picture of a hospital ward. Angela was crying, head pushed into the pillow. Eric had rushed through the set of double doors, having only just made it there, once everything was over.

"There were... complications," the doctor told him before he went in. "We did our best."

"Thank you," Eric told him. "I'm sure you did."

When Angela saw him, she sniffed back the tears. "Where have you *been*, Eric? Where were you?"

"I'm so sorry. The orphanage—"

"The orphanage!" Angela let out a wail. "You were with those... those... When your own child..." She couldn't speak anymore, turning away again and crying into the pillow. The Eric of yesteryear reached out his hand to place it on her shoulder, but then withdrew it.

The Eric from the present was crying freely, but the spirit wasn't about to let him off that easily. "It didn't end there, though, did it? In spite of this, you carried on, spending more and more time away from home. Away from Angela."

"No!"

"Oh yes," argued the ghost, showing him the photo he'd dreaded most. The one of Angela sitting alone on Christmas Day, still in the same flat they'd owned years before, two plates of dinner on the table in front of her. And where had Eric been?

"I was... I needed to—"

"You were helping those who couldn't help themselves. I know."

As Eric continued to watch, Angela rose and picked up the phone, dialling a number. "It's me," she said down the line. "Can I come over? I need you. I need to be with you."

Eric was crying again, the anger welling in him. "You..." he almost said "bastard", changing it at the last second to, "Bugger."

The ghost spared him the sight of Angela in the arms of another man, thankfully ("He was everything *you* showed the promise of being: exciting, going places. He wasn't the first, and wouldn't be the last, of course. But they all shared that common trait, Eric. While you tried to save the world, staying stock still at the same time."). But what he did show Eric was so much worse.

A final photograph, and this one had Eric serving some ragged men at the soup kitchens as he did every year. He watched himself doling out the hot broth and the kind words in equal measures, then looked over at the ghost as if to ask why he was showing him this. How could it possibly change his mind – this was what he was meant to do, what Jared had inspired him to do.

Jared. This was all connected to him. Because, as they watched, those same men left the kitchens and walked the streets. Eric and the ghost saw them notice a man strolling down the road wearing a suit and raincoat, carrying a holdall. Eric watched in horror as the men he'd just helped nudged each other, nodding across at the guy, then following until they spotted a good place to jump him.

But Jared was reluctant to part with the holdall, and they saw why when they yanked it from his hand and got a look inside at all the cash.

"No, you leave that alone. It belongs to—" The man's cries were silenced with a knife to the stomach, but one blow obviously wasn't enough, because they kept on ramming the blade into him, over and over. Leaving him bleeding red against the slushy white snow.

Then they ran off, leaving Jared Marlowe in the gutter to die.

Eric fell backwards, a hand to his mouth. Fell back out of the photograph and into his flat. He was trembling, in shock from the knowledge that the people he'd been trying to help, to feed at this special time of year, had thrown it back in his face – murdering his best friend in the whole world.

"Jared," said Eric, not able to take the information in.

And he was still reeling when the next supernatural visitor arrived in his home.

~

The Second of the Three Spirits

It took Eric a moment or so to realise that the thing had appeared under the tree.

But it was big, so big in fact it dwarfed the tree itself and he almost fell backwards over it, stumbling to bat away the visions that the sepia-toned ghost had brought him.

Eric wiped his eyes and stared at the box.

It was brightly coloured, all reds and golds and greens, wrapped up with the greatest of care and tied with a bow on the top. As with the buzzer downstairs, the last thing Eric had been expecting it to do was talk.

"Don't just stand there lookin' at me, then," said the box, jiggling; the voice this time was fairly gruff, in direct opposition to the one from before. "Open me up!"

"What... who...?" Eric began.

The box let out a groan. "Isn't it *obvious* who I am?"

"Erm... Not really."

"I'm a bleedin' Christmas Present," said the box, jiggling again. "Think about it."

Eric frowned. He had no idea what this had to do with what Jared had told him at the start. He didn't need any presents, especially one that was *telling* him he needed it.

"Well, come on then. What's wrong with you? Most people like to open Christmas Presents."

To be honest, it had been so long since anyone had given Eric a gift at this time of year, he'd forgotten the procedure. His usually came in the form of a smile from someone he'd helped.

"Don't be so bloody wet," the present sniped. "Get your arse down here and get openin' me. *Right now!*" The voice sounded so much like his boss, Mr Fitzgerald, that Eric instinctively did as he was told, getting on his hands and knees and pulling at the bow. It came away easily, as did the paper on the top – like it was helping Eric itself to get it open; which, in all likelihood, it was. Eric opened up the box itself, curious – having come this far – to see what was inside.

It was a box, wrapped just as intricately as the last one. Eric heard gruff laughter.

"What is this?"

"It's another present," came the reply. "So go on, open it."

Eric felt stupid, and he felt duped. But that curiosity hadn't left him, plus this game was at least taking his mind off the things he'd just witnessed thanks to the sepia-coloured spirit. He undid this parcel too, only to find... another box.

"Heh-heh-heh," came the laughter again.

"You've got to be kidding."

"I am and I'm not," said the Present. "Half the fun of opening me is the expectation, so I like to tease it out a little. Don't worry, it'll be worth it."

Eric's head lolled. "I doubt that very much."

"What if I said you could sell what's in me, raise some money for charity. If you must."

That got Eric's attention. Not that he fully trusted what this or the other ghosts had told him tonight. But it was worth having a peek inside the present just to make sure. If there was a way of making some money here – to feed and clothe the needy, of course – then he owed it to them to continue.

"All right," Eric said, diving in again, ignoring the laughter.

This went on for some time, a smaller present inside each of the presents he was opening. Like Russian dolls, he placed them in a row on the floor of his flat. There were ten in total, and when Eric finally came to the last of them, he looked over to see that they'd formed themselves into a rough figure beside him, held together with the wrapping and bows, which also created the illusion of a face. This only fazed him for a moment (after all it was no more strange than a person made of photographs) and then Eric undid the final present.

"Aha!" he said, taking out his reward. "Paydirt!"

The Present hadn't lied after all, because in here was a top of the line, compact Handycam. Had to be worth at least a couple of hundred pounds, if not more. Eric was just glad this hadn't been here when he'd been robbed.

As he took it out, he saw a red light flashing on the side of it. The blessed thing had been accidentally turned on before being wrapped up. Eric turned it over and over in his hands, looking for the way to switch it off again. He opened up the viewing screen on the side, hopeful that the button might be concealed inside. But as his eyes caught the screen, he was surprised to see that the image being recorded didn't match the scene in front of him. The camera should have been picking up the tree, the edge of the window, the cracked plaster of the walls. Instead there was another room entirely: a much bigger, finer room. Eric waved his hand in front of the lens, but the camera failed to pick it up.

"What's going on here?" he asked.

"Why don't you have a closer look and see?" replied the Present in that rough voice, and in spite of himself Eric did, putting the viewfinder up to his eye. It was like looking through one of those magic tubes when he was a kid, seeing a picture that he knew shouldn't be there at the other end. Only this one was moving. Someone came into shot and Eric's eyes trailed them: a woman, wearing a long, flowing silken gown. She was beautiful, hair expertly coiffured, face perfectly made up – red lipstick covering her pouting mouth. She had the kind of lashes that could blow a man away... in more ways than one.

As she moved around the enormous room, Eric took more of it in. There were paintings on the wall, and though he was no expert he suspected these were the real deal: a Constable, a Landseer, even a Monet. Any one of them would be able to fund the refuge for months, maybe even years. There was a roaring fire under one of the paintings, the mantel covered in cards, with a clock in the middle. There was a grand piano situated in the far corner of the room, next to a set of marble steps, and two bookcases along the back wall, full of the kind of tomes he'd lost tonight (though Eric suspected the owners hardly touched them; like everything else here, they were for show – to show *how* incredibly rich and powerful these people were). In the other corner was a Christmas tree so tall it reached the high ceiling, covered in lights and baubles, with a gigantic fairy planted on the top.

As the woman drifted across the space, feet covered by the robe so that she herself resembled a ghost, Eric felt a sudden pang of jealousy. *No, he said to himself. They're just* things. *Material goods that you can do without. It's* people *who are important.*

"Why are you showing me this?" Eric asked the new ghost. It didn't make any sense. He didn't even know this woman, didn't recognise this place. He felt seedy, like some kind of voyeur.

"Keep watching," replied the spirit. "You'll see."

Eric did as he was told and as he watched, he saw a man come into view. A portly fellow he knew all too well. It was his boss, Mr Fitzgerald. The man waddled down the steps, holding onto the rail for support, passing the piano and joining the woman on the massive couch in the centre of the room. Two of the biggest, comfiest chairs Eric had ever seen flanked this, and all of them were covered in the most expensive dark leather – waxed so much that it was a wonder people didn't just slide off the seats.

So that's it, all this belongs to him, *paid for by his cutthroat and underhand work dealings.*

Fitzgerald kissed the woman on the cheek, slobbering over her and squeezing into the gap – his huge girth initially proving a stumbling block to sitting comfortably. Eric realised this must be Fitzgerald's wife, Vanora. He'd heard some of the other office workers talking about her every now and again: about how she was Fitzgerald's fifth spouse; about how she was a former model and beauty queen (he could believe that now); about how it had been the money rather than Fitzgerald's other 'charms' that had attracted her. Nevertheless, Eric also knew that there had been a product of this union, as mind-judderingly disturbing as that was to imagine (so Eric chose not to). A young boy about the same age as his own child would have—

Eric mentally shook his head, telling himself not to go there again.

As if on cue, and preventing Fitzgerald from becoming any more amorous with this wife – which nobody needed to see – a small boy in pyjamas came down the steps, laughing.

"Now, Tommy, you know it's way past your bedtime," said Vanora. "Santa won't come and leave you any presents if you're not a good little boy."

Tommy looked at her sideways, as if about to question whether Santa existed at all, but decided not to chance it and came over to give his parents a hug and kiss before heading back off to bed. When he walked across, Eric noticed the boy had a slight limp.

"What's wrong with him?" he asked the Present.

"There were... complications at his birth," replied the gruff voice. "But he pulled through. He's a tough little cookie. Plus, he had the finest doctors money could buy helping him through it."

Eric was silent. He watched Tommy jump up on Fitzgerald's lap, wondering what that feeling might have been like. To have been a Dad to such a lovely little tyke. Fitzgerald, however, looked like he couldn't wait to get rid of his son – probably so he could get his hands on Vanora again.

Vanora gave her son a kiss and then told him to get off back to bed and go straight to sleep. "There's a good boy," she added.

As soon as Tommy was gone, Fitzgerald was slobbering over his wife again, this time his hand riding up her gown. He muttered something about giving her an early present, and that's when Eric pulled the viewfinder back down from his eye.

"Ugh," he said. But the image of the house, of the life his boss was living, remained with him. Surely Fitzgerald didn't deserve such happiness, did he? After all the dishonest things he'd done, all the people he'd screwed over? Though Eric felt bad for thinking it, there was also a part of him that resented Fitzgerald for having Tommy; that felt like the boy should have been his.

"He played the game," said the Present. "Built up his business – through whatever means – and now he's reaping the benefits."

"I didn't say a thing," Eric replied, but then he didn't need to. With these guys it was enough to just think it. He looked down and saw that the image on the viewscreen had changed, thankfully. It now showed his nephew, Fraser, with a couple of other youths his age, hitting the town on Christmas Eve.

Curiosity got the better of him again, and Eric pressed his eye to the viewfinder. He watched as the lads entered a club, a techno beat throbbing in the background. They ordered at the bar and began drinking their lagers.

"Look familiar?" asked the Present. "This was how *you* used to have a good time before you became such a stiff."

Eric ignored him, concentrating on what Fraser was up to. He and his mates had already spotted some girls in the corner wearing skimpy green elf outfits and had gone over to begin chatting them up. Fraser was much cooler and much better at it than Eric had ever been, and within minutes he was up and dancing with one of the women: a very attractive brunette whose hat flopped from side to side as she gyrated around Fraser. It wasn't long before she had her arms wrapped round him, and he was whispering in her ear. Next thing her tongue was down his throat, so far it looked like she was trying to clean his Adam's apple. Eric pulled a face, feigning disgust – but in reality he wondered what it would be like to be kissed again, to have someone pay him attention in that way again. It got very lonely inside his flat all on his own.

"It's your choice," the Present reminded him. "This is Fraser most weekends, out on the town – and on the pull."

"I'm not sure I want to know."

"Aww, leave him alone. He's young, free and single. He's also seriously loaded. He could have any woman he wanted. And he frequently does!" As the Present was talking, and as if to demonstrate, Fraser was leading the elf outside where they climbed into a taxi – and promptly began snogging again on the backseat as it transported them to his place.

Eric raised an eyebrow when he saw Fraser's pad. He knew the lad was doing all right, but this was something else. An exclusive top floor apartment with balcony, the place was kitted out with all the latest mod cons and an interior that looked like the inside of a spaceship: all white walls and chrome. Fraser's TV alone covered most of one wall, a digital flatscreen which he flicked on to one of the music channels as he fixed the elf another drink from his well-stocked bar.

"Wow!" Eric exclaimed.

"I know," said the Present.

Not long after, Fraser took the dark-haired elf off by the hand and into the bedroom. Again, Eric moved the camera down before he could see any more. He hadn't wanted to see Fitzgerald at it, let alone his own nephew. The young man's lifestyle, though, had made Eric think. He'd always maintained that Fraser was wasting his life away: the clubs, the drinking, the casual sex. But wasn't he only making the most of his time on this planet? If Jared was right – and Eric still wasn't convinced of that – then which one of the two of them was actually making the most of this gift called life?

"That's easy," said the Present, answering the rhetorical question. "*Him.*"

Eric shook his head, he'd had enough of this. He was just about to put down the camera for good when his eyes caught the viewing screen again. It was no longer throwing back an image of Fraser and the girl. Now it was showing him something altogether different.

"Angela?" he said.

"Angela," confirmed the Present.

She was sitting alone at a table again, in a place that looked not dissimilar to the flat they'd once shared together. But instead of a turkey dinner in front of her there was a half-empty bottle of gin. Eric pressed his eye up to the viewfinder, just as she opened her clenched right hand. She was holding a selection of different coloured pills, sitting there staring at them through tear-stained eyes.

"No…" breathed Eric. "Don't show me this."

"It's my final present to you. She's all alone again, Eric. Those other guys never stuck around for very long." The Present's voice grew even deeper. "She could be yours again. You could save her. All you'd have to do would be to become the man you always should have been.

The man she *thought* she was marrying in the first place."

Oh, that was low. Eric gritted his teeth, shook his head again. No, he wouldn't be blackmailed, not even when he wanted Angela back as much as he did. He threw the camera across the room. It smashed to pieces on the already cracked wall.

"There's just no pleasing some people, is there?" grumbled the Christmas Present Ghost. "I wish I'd just bought you socks instead now."

And before Eric's eyes, the wrapping paper and bows separated, causing the box figure to fall apart and collapse right there in front of him.

~

The Third of the Three Spirits

Eric remained on his knees for some time; he felt like a broken man.

He'd discovered that not only was there nothing whatsoever on the other side – not even if you'd devoted yourself to helping your fellow man – but if he'd taken a different route in the past not only might he still have a wife, he'd probably have a child as well (once again, the image of little Tommy coming down those steps flashed across his mind). What's more, he'd been shown that his best friend had died at the hands of people he himself had been kind to, plus his ex was about to top herself because of the car wreck her life had become... All because of him.

So engrossed in his misery was Eric that he hadn't noticed he was in almost complete darkness now that the ghosts had departed. It was appropriate somehow, reflected how he felt inside. But this was no ordinary gloom, as he soon discovered when it reached out and touched him on the shoulder. Eric started, rising and spinning around to try and catch sight of whatever was out there. He saw nothing, couldn't even see the hand in front of his face.

"Who's there?"

No reply. If it was the third and final ghost of the evening, then he'd at least expected it to give some smart arse reply like the others. He asked once more, and again there was no answer.

The darkness tapped him on the other shoulder and he spun around in a different direction. If he'd been thinking straight he would have wondered how he hadn't fallen over something, or hit a wall by now. "This is not funny," Eric complained. "If you're here for me, then just get on with it, will you?"

An outline revealed itself, faint and still part of the blackness. Eric squinted; it looked very much to him like a cloak and hood, but he couldn't see any hint of a face. Still without saying anything, the third ghost did as it was instructed and 'got on with it'.

Ironically, the whole thing started off as a faint light this time – bright against the darkness. Then a series of lights, like lasers, shooting out of the black and projecting an image. An image that soon became 3D, wrapping itself around Eric like something out of a futuristic SF movie by James Cameron.

Eric found himself looking at an office. An empty chair in an office, to be precise. *His* empty chair at the office. But that was all right, this was Christmas Day, had to be – he could tell from the sparse decorations Fitzgerald allowed. And nobody worked there on Christmas Day... Except today they were. Wendy from accounts, Roy manning the phones, Dave walking around with a piece of paper in his hand as always, trying to look busy but actually not doing very much. All acquaintances rather than actual friends; they simply couldn't understand any of Eric's obsessions.

They looked thoroughly miserable, and as Eric listened in he discovered why. All his work colleagues were moaning about the fact that Fitzgerald had made them come in. "'There are plenty more people who'd be glad of the job if you're not'," said Wendy, doing a pretty decent imitation of her boss – who was no doubt at home enjoying his day with his wife and kid.

"But where am *I*?" asked Eric.

Once again, the ghost who was there but not really there gave no reply. Eric heard his name and tuned back in to the conversation.

"He's better off," Dave said. "Least he's not slaving away."

Eric frowned. There was something about the way they were talking about him, something so very final. He swallowed hard. "So that's it. I'm dead, right? Is that what you're trying to tell me? I haven't got long so make the most of it?"

The hologram show blurred then and created another image. It was Eric, though he had to look really closely to recognise himself. He was sitting in a shop doorway, huddling against the cold. He had a long, matted and greying beard, to match his long, matted and greying hair. His clothes were virtually rags, held together with bits of string, and his shoes had more holes in them than a piece of Swiss cheese. *Right,* thought Eric, *so I lose my job. And it looks like my flat as well. How?*

"Spare us some change," the older Eric pleaded, holding out his hand. But people were walking by, ignoring him. He hung his head in despair.

Eric watched as the version of him from the future got up, heading to the refuge where he'd once given so much of his time. Except he was stopped at the door by someone he didn't recognise – a volunteer who must have come along since his time there – and told that they were full.

"But I used to help out here," future Eric argued. "I gave all my money to places like this, to causes like this one. It's Christmas, for Heaven's sake! Have some pity."

The man just told him to get lost because he was stinking up the place.

Shaking his head, Eric shambled away.

So that was it: he was destined to become one of the people he'd helped, destitute and unloved. Where the hell was Fraser? That's what he wanted to know. His only family left in the world?

He watched as the hologram shimmered again and showed Eric a picture of himself hiding behind a wall, near a cash machine. Waiting for a lone man with a bunch of flowers in his hand to finish withdrawing his money. When he got close enough, the future Eric jumped out and attempted to snatch his wallet. The man resisted and Eric didn't appear to have the strength to fight him. More bystanders rushed towards the struggling pair so Eric cut his losses and ran. The present-day Eric next saw him hiding behind some bins, breathing hard and crying.

He wanted to as well.

The hologram shifted its perspective again and showed Eric his older self staggering along a train station platform. He watched as the ragged man he would become took out a photo from his pocket. Eric walked around himself, to see who was in it. He might have guessed. It was Angela, probably dead some years by now.

"Don't do it," he told himself, but he knew by now the man couldn't hear. "*Please*," he continued anyway.

The train was coming, too fast to be stopping at the station. Eric reached out to try and stop his future self from jumping in front of it, but of course it did no good.

Eric closed his eyes, refusing to look. But then he heard the sound of Fraser's voice. He looked again to see the hologram had settled on one final scene: Fraser, a few years older judging by the lines on his face and receding hairline, standing over a grave, tears in his eyes.

"Oh Uncle, why didn't you call me? Why did we drift apart like this?" said Fraser. "I wish you'd stayed in touch."

So that was it, *he'd* been the one who'd shunned Fraser – just like he'd blown him off that very day. His only relation.

Eric came round and stood beside Fraser, looking down at the gravestone his nephew must have bought. He'd been an idiot, a fool for all these years. But what could he do to prevent all this?

"I *have* to know, are these the events of what will be or what might be?" he asked.

Predictably, there was no answer.

But, seconds later, the hologram lightshow folded in on itself, and blackness returned. He couldn't tell for sure but he suspected the ghost had gone, if it had even been here at all. Perhaps it had been his own subconscious, and if it really had been a dream then that was trying to tell him something as well.

Eric sat up on his sofa-bed – where he'd begun this adventure – a changed man.

He was determined to do something about his life, about his attitude. He was going to get back his edge, get back Angela, and somehow make his mark. Eric hadn't figured it all out yet, but it would somehow involve Fraser dishing up the dirt on Fitzgerald (when he was in charge of that company, Eric would make sure the employees got their Christmas Day off at least, though not a second more. He would also throw his ex-boss a bone of a lowly office job; well, he didn't want to see poor Tommy out on the streets).

All thoughts of getting up to help at the soup kitchen vanquished from his mind, Eric plotted and planned and schemed: not least of which how he was going to get his leatherbound books back, with the help of either a few of his less savoury neighbours or some of the folk he'd come into contact with helping the homeless (he could think of a couple of excellent replacements for the 'muscle' of his childhood friends).

The spirits had taught him much, and all in one night. He would put it to good use, and make the most of the time he had left...

~

Jared Marlowe observed his old friend from the safety of the otherworld.

His plan had worked beautifully, even if he did say so himself. He'd done what so many others had failed to do in the past, putting right a wrong that had taken place so many years ago, to Eric's ancestor. If the 'powers that be' hadn't interfered back then, Eric's line would have carried on being the cruelty and misery poster boys for evil that had been intended. But oh no, *They* couldn't have that – so They'd brainwashed old Ebenezer into being good, and kind. At least that's the version of the story Jared had been told.

Told by his new master. The one he'd done the deal with.

He'd been lying, of course, when he said there was nothing after death. There *were* sides, obviously, and Jared – after a lifetime of stealing, cheating and conning people – had found himself on the wrong one. Or the right one, as it now happened. Did he feel guilty about the way he'd manipulated his old mate, Eric? No more than he did about deceiving him in the first place – about letting him believe that he'd been murdered by homeless people Eric had helped, when in actual fact it had been the mob he'd been on his way to give the charity money to; paying off some of his own gambling debts (though he hadn't had quite enough to stop them from doing what they did).

He'd actually done Eric a favour in the long run, if he thought about it. All that do-gooding was fine, but he'd have much more fun this way (though not as much fun as Jared had been promised if he could pull this off). He might also be happier, or so Jared told himself. He chose not to think about the many people Eric had helped – inspired by his own supposedly good deeds, which were nothing of the sort (he'd never bloody well asked Eric to emulate him, had he) – or *would have* helped in the future. It just meant that there was more chance they'd see each other again after Eric did eventually shuffle off his mortal coil.

Eric had finally been allowed to keep Christmas in his own way, just as his ancestor wanted to. Jared grinned, knowing he had escaped his fate because of all that he'd achieved – the thought of those flames, those chains and hooks made him shudder – and that his stunt here would be the stuff of legend in the years to come. Who knows, maybe they'd even write about it one day?

Jared wondered what they might call the tale if they ever did.

Perhaps a variation of what Eric's ancestor had once used as his catchphrase, something to emphasise how the Scrooge family had been well and truly screwed by those kiss-ass spirits before (he preferred his own versions much better).

Yes, that seems appropriate, thought Jared Marlowe, whistling merrily as he returned to the hot realm below that he now called home.

Rubbing his hands in anticipation of his own Christmas futures to come.

I don't really know what happened.

One minute the way ahead of me was clear – I mean clear like on a spring day – the next I was in the middle of it and everything was white. It was like a giant hand had just shaken an Earth snow globe, and I was stuck in the middle.

The crystals descended on my windscreen like miniature parachutists, each one sacrificing itself upon impact; their mission to obscure my vision. *Christ!* All the forecasters said that the snow was going to hold off until at least the following week, yet there I was in the thick of a veritable blizzard. Then again, when was the last time they'd ever been right about anything?

It was my own fault, really. I should have listened to my girlfriend – stayed at home with her over the holiday period instead of bailing out after Boxing Day.

"We're not all freelancers, Carrie," I'd said to her. "Some of us have to work when we're told."

"They promised you a week, Adam." She'd folded her arms, slumping down on the couch amidst the detritus of wrapping paper and boxes we hadn't cleared away yet.

"I know, I know… but one of their branches up north is having problems with the new system. Jacobs wants me to go and sort it."

"Adam—"

"Look, I don't want to lose my job. Not in this climate." (There were worse, as I found out.) "I'll be back in a couple of days, I promise. Then I'll make it up to you." I leaned in for a kiss, but she turned away, pouting. I'm not sure, but I thought I saw tears welling in her eyes. *Congratulations*, I said to myself, *you've managed to ruin the entire festive season*. And after we'd had such a nice time, at that.

Didn't stop me going, though. I had to, it was my job; times were hard and we were saving for a new place. What had she expected me to do? Tell Jacobs to go screw himself? She'd get over it, I told myself. I'd soon be back and then we could pick up where we'd left off, have a nice New Year's then look forward to the future. I'd make it up to her somehow; it was what I always told myself when I headed off.

Only at that moment, a warm inviting fire and Carrie's arms around me seemed infinitely more appealing than driving through this shit to the arse end of nowhere, along country lanes that were probably just as dangerous before the snow started coming down. And for what? So I could fix a few bugs in some computer. *Probably only needs turning off and on again*, I thought, allowing myself a little smile even though I was worried. I'd never driven in conditions as bad as this before. From what little I could see, the road was completely covered, inches piling up and making it hard for my Dunlops to find purchase. Oh, what I wouldn't have given for a gritter lorry right about then. I slowed down and changed gears. The wipers on my car were clogged with snow, jerking their way across the glass in fits and starts.

By this time it was snowing so hard, the wind blowing it straight at me, that I didn't notice the bend – such as it was. I was only doing about fifteen miles an hour at most, and the kink in the road was only at a slight angle, but my car immediately began skidding and I ended up in a ditch, slamming into it with all the force of a rally driving casualty. The seatbelt caught me, but I still banged my arm and forehead on the steering wheel. I don't mind admitting it shook me up pretty badly, though I realised even at the time it could have been a lot worse. My hands didn't stop shaking for five minutes afterwards, and when I tried to start the dead engine, it dawned on me that I was probably a good ten miles or more from the nearest town. Even if I could somehow breathe life into my Escort, I'd have a devil of a job trying to get out of this ditch.

My next thought was to call for help. I grabbed my mobile from the passenger seat where I always keep it when I'm driving, casually slinging it on there after taking it out of my pocket – little realising that it might, one day, be my only connection to the outside world. I breathed a sigh of relief when I saw the battery was full, but it soon turned to one of despair when I saw the signal bar was giving me nothing. Nevertheless, I tried – but only got an angry bleeping for my trouble. I couldn't reach anyone, RAC, police, fire brigade – the bloody Household Cavalry.

Or Carrie... Oh, how I wanted to hear her voice then.

I threw the phone back down, not caring now that it was my only potential lifeline. It bounced off the seat and smashed against the glove compartment, splitting in two in the process.

"Shit!" I picked it up, putting it together again. But now I couldn't even get the screen to come on. If it wasn't reaching civilisation before, there was no hope now. I tried not to panic. Maybe if I just sat here a little while, someone would come along.

Who? A shepherd checking on his snow-covered flock?

I probably wasn't the only one to get caught in this freak storm, but I was betting I was the only person stupid or unlucky enough to get caught in it *out here*. In fact, I'd chosen this route exactly because I didn't want to run into any traffic. Come to think of it, I'd barely seen a soul since I took the exit off the motorway, and that was a good hour ago. Even if a driver was idiotic enough to be out here in the middle of the holidays, *and it was possible* I told myself, they probably wouldn't see my car in the ditch. Already the snow had built up over my bonnet, mounting my windscreen and obliterating every inch of paintwork. Slowly and surely, I was being entombed in this metallic coffin.

With the heaters now gone, it was getting steadily colder. I reached in the back for my coat and quickly pulled it on, starting to shiver as I did so. I had no gloves with me, so I jammed my hands down in my pockets as far as they'd go without ripping the lining.

It was becoming clear I had to do something. As time ticked away and the snow fell harder and harder, I started to lose the slim hope that someone might come along. My only options were to sit there and turn into an icicle, or try to make it to a main road of some description. Now, I know the emergency services tell you to stay in your car at times like these, but I'm sure they never have exactly this situation in mind when they issue such warnings.

The door would hardly budge at first and I was frightened I might have left it too late. But, with a bit of effort, and some shoulder power, I managed to force open a gap so I could get out. Everything was totally white outside: the sky; the ground; the fields. My breath turned instantly to steam as I panted, leaning up against the car. I looked at a road map I'd brought out with me, which gave me some idea of the direction to take, although a compass would have been nice. Everything looked the same now, it was so disorientating.

I was just about to set off when I saw the lights. God knows how they cut through the whiteness, I just assumed – prayed – they belonged to a vehicle of some kind. Preferably with bloody great tractor wheels. They glared brighter and brighter, those lights, at one point threatening to outdo the snow.

Then they just vanished.

I shouted, waved my hands, desperate to attract the attention of whoever had been pointing those beams in my direction. It would be just my luck for that car to have crashed as well – though the more I thought about it, could it have been something like a helicopter? But out in this? It would explain why the lights suddenly disappeared; they'd drifted away... or crashed themselves. I was focussing so intently on the area in front, I never noticed the figures behind me. Not until one of them put a hand on my shoulder.

I jumped at the touch, nearly toppling sideways into a snow bank.

"I'm sorry, I didn't mean to startle you." The man spoke with a tired voice, every word an effort. He was about my height, but thinning on top, and wore a grey suit that was wet in places. Cowering behind him was a boy, about half his size. He looked about ten, and his features so closely resembled the man's that it had to be his son. Both were shivering so much their teeth were chattering.

"No... no, that's all right," I said holding up my hand. "I mean, I'm just glad someone's found me." I was babbling, so pleased to see another person I could have hugged him. "Was that your car? The headlights?" I asked.

The man shook his head. "Our car's stuck about half a mile down the road. We've just been walking, trying to find a house or somewhere with a phone."

So they were just as helpless as me – didn't even have a mobile, by the sounds of it. "Jesus, you two look freezing." The man's skin was a light shade of blue, and despite the colour in his son's cheeks – he looked like he'd been slapped hard round the face – I could see the blood there was cooling in this rapidly dropping temperature. "Hold on a minute, I think there might be a couple of pac-a-macs in the front here." I'd bought them on holiday in Wales a few years back when it looked like storms overhead, and thinking about that made me think of Carrie again. I shook away the memories, and searched for the macs – at least they would keep the pair dry, if not warm. Both father and son seemed grateful, judging from the smiles I received.

"I'm Harry Sharpe and this is my boy, Tim." We shook hands, strangers thrown together by circumstance.

"Adam. Adam Riley, though I don't seem to be living his life right now..." I gave a small laugh, but Harry just stared at me blankly. There was silence then, neither party sure what to do or say. But *something* needed to be done.

"Well, we can't just stand around here," said the man as if reading my thoughts. "I say we go on until we find somewhere or somebody."

I nodded, not really wanting to leave, but not wanting to stay either. So I said my goodbyes to the snowbound Escort and we all pushed onwards, into the driving winter storm.

Now, I've seen film footage of men trekking across the arctic or wherever, braving the elements in search of fame and glory, but I don't think even they could have come up against the conditions we saw that dreadful Wednesday in December. God, or whoever was in charge, was certainly taking his anger out on the world that day – laying waste to nature and wildlife alike – and we were caught in the crossfire.

My face was chapped by the icy wind, and I was continually batting flakes of snow from my eyes. Harry fell, twice, into the snow by the side of the road (not that you could really see the sides anymore) and had to be helped up. Each time, Tim looked at me with anxious eyes. If we didn't find help soon...

And again, I saw the lights, those round headlamps, but moving so fast. Couldn't possibly be a plough or one of those gritter lorries I'd been praying for. It didn't matter, they disappeared just as quickly, just like the last time. Before I could get a good look at them, or they at us.

On, into the sleet we went, walking for what seemed like forever. I put my arm round Harry's shoulder, and I held Tim's hand as we went, looking for all the world like battle-torn infantrymen from some great war.

As we trudged further, Harry spoke of how

he wanted to see his wife again. How he wished she were here so he could tell her one more time that he loved her.

"Don't talk like that, mate. You'll see her," I told him, but there was very little conviction in my voice. And his words made me think of Carrie again; how I might become lost in this blank wilderness and never hold her again, never look into her beautiful eyes.

"I – I'm sorry," managed Harry. "I just can't go on." I could barely hear him now above the coarse winds.

"You have to..."

"No, you go. Find help."

"I can't leave you here like this," I said, but his hand was waving me away. I knew it would be dark soon, and his only chance would be if I could bring back help. He looked at me and I nodded. Tim wouldn't leave his father behind and I didn't have time to make him. All I could do was leave my coat for them to huddle under. They needed it more than I did.

I staggered away from them, turning only as I took my ninth or tenth step. They looked distant through the snow, melding with the blizzard, and that light again.

What the hell *was* that light?

I tried to run, in spite of the fact the snow came up to my knees. I stumbled, hand held out in front as the light seemed to be coming from all directions at once. I understood now that it wasn't headlights, or a helicopter – there were millions of lights, illuminating the dots of snow.

I must have been hallucinating, delirious, because each flake took on a shape suddenly. A figure with wings, and a glowing face; radiant snow angels. The light was growing stronger and I thought I saw two familiar faces in one flurry – Harry and Tim, still huddled together – before the stark white was replaced by an all-consuming black.

I woke crying out for help, and gentle hands eased me back down onto the bed. Carrie was there in the hospital by my side.

At first I thought it was another hallucination. I'd wanted to see her so much out there in the snowstorm. But she was real enough, and so was the broad smile on her face as she held my hand tightly.

"Oh God, I thought I'd lost you. When they rang to say..." There were tears in her eyes again, but these were ones of joy.

"Carrie, listen to me." I tried to raise myself up, but she prevented me again. She's always been quite strong, and I was in no shape to argue.

"Easy sweetheart... take it easy. You've been through a lot."

"You have to help them, Carrie. *Please*, they're still out there!"

Carrie frowned. "Who, baby?"

"They're lost in the snow, like I was."

A young doctor was there with Carrie, looking me over. "Please try to relax, Mr Riley. You've been in an accident. Your car went off the road and you were found up on a hillside quite a way from the scene. There was no-one else with you, I'm afraid."

"Please, we... you have to go and look for them. The blizzard—"

"Adam, sweetheart..." Carrie stroked my hair back. "There hasn't been any snow yet this year. It's clear skies and actually quite warm out there."

The doctor nodded. "She's right. The last blizzard we had around here was a good fifteen, twenty years ago. A real snowstorm it was; I was only a kid but I remember it well. You're lucky you weren't out in something like that. Couple of people even died as I recall."

I stared, open-mouthed. How could it be blue skies and sun outside, it didn't make sense? And where were Harry and—

I shook my head. No, it couldn't be. It was too crazy to even think about. The storm, the people who'd died. I looked at the doctor, but didn't need to ask him the names of the victims who'd perished out there in the last blizzard. In fact, it was probably better for my sanity if I didn't.

I could put it all down to the bump on the head, if I wanted to, but that was too easy an explanation. It had felt real, the cold. My arm around Harry's shoulders, holding Tim's hand, just like Carrie was holding mine.

I squeezed it tightly, remembering what Harry had said about seeing his wife and knew he never did.

And I thought about the snow, what I'd seen in it. The moment when those snow angels had come for that father and son.

The moment when they'd claimed them as their own.

Also by Paul Kane:

Novels
Arrowhead (Abaddon, 2008)
Broken Arrow (Abaddon, 2009)
Arrowland (Abaddon, 2010)
Hooded Man (Omnibus) (Abaddon, 2013)
The Gemini Factor (Screaming Dreams, 2010)
Of Darkness and Light (Thunderstorm Books, 2010)
Lunar (Bad Moon Books, 2012)
Sleeper(s) (Crystal Lake Publishing, 2013)
The Rainbow Man (as P.B. Kane) (Rocket Ride Books, 2013)
Blood RED (SST Publications, 2015)
Sherlock Holmes and the Servants of Hell (Solaris Books, 2016)
Before (Grey Matter Press, 2017)

Novellas & Novelettes
Signs of Life (Crystal Serenades, 2005)
The Lazarus Condition (Tasmaniac Publications, 2007)
Dalton Quayle Rides Out (Pendragon Press, 2007)
RED (Skullvines Press, 2008)
Pain Cages (Books of the Dead, 2011)

Creakers (chapbook) (Spectral Press, 2013)
The Curse of the Wolf (Hersham Horror Books, 2014)
Flaming Arrow (Abaddon, 2015)
The P.I.'s Tale (2016)
Snow (Stormblade Productions, 2016)
End of the End (Abaddon, 2016)
The Crimson Mystery (SST, 2016)
The Rot (Horrific Tales, 2016)
Beneath the Surface (with Simon Clark) (SST, 2017)

Collections

Alone (In the Dark) (BJM Press, 2001)
Touching the Flame (Rainfall Books, 2002)
FunnyBones (Creative Guy Publications, 2003)
Peripheral Visions (Creative Guy Publications, 2008)
The Adventures of Dalton Quayle (Mundania Press, 2011)
Shadow Writer (Mansion House Books, 2011)
The Butterfly Man and Other Stories (PS Publishing, 2011)
The Spaces Between (Dark Moon Books, 2013)
Ghosts (Spectral Press, 2013)
Monsters (Alchemy Press, 2015)
The Dead Trilogy (NewCon Press, 2016)

Shadow Casting (SST Publications, 2016)
Nailbiters (as Paul B Kane) (Black Shuck Books, 2017)
Death (The Sinister Horror Company, 2017)
Disexistence (Cycatrix Press, 2017)

Non-Fiction
The Hellraiser Films And Their Legacy (McFarland)
Voices in the Dark (McFarland, 2010)
Shadow Writer – The Non-Fiction. Vol. 1: Reviews (BearManor Media)
Shadow Writer – The Non-Fiction. Vol. 2: Articles & Essays (BearManor Media)

Visit Paul Kane at his website:
www.shadow-writer.co.uk

Shadows 9 – Winter Freits
> by Andrew David Barker

Shadows 10 – The Dead
> by Paul Kane

Shadows 11 – The Forest of Dead Children
> by Andrew Hook

Shadows 12 – At Home in the Shadows
> by Gary McMahon

blackshuckbooks.co.uk/shadows